Written and illustrated by Marty Kelley.

Kelley, Marty
    The Rules / by Marty Kelley
       p. cm.
    Summary: A rhyming survey of many things that adults tell children to do and not to do.
    ISBN 1-55933-284-0
    [1. Behavior -fiction. 2. Stories in rhyme.] I. Title.
    PZ8.3.K298 Ru 2000
    [E] -dc21

                                                        00-035402

10 9 8 7 6 5 4
First Printing September 2000

Delyla -
BE GOOD!
Marty Kelley

the rules

by
marty
kelley

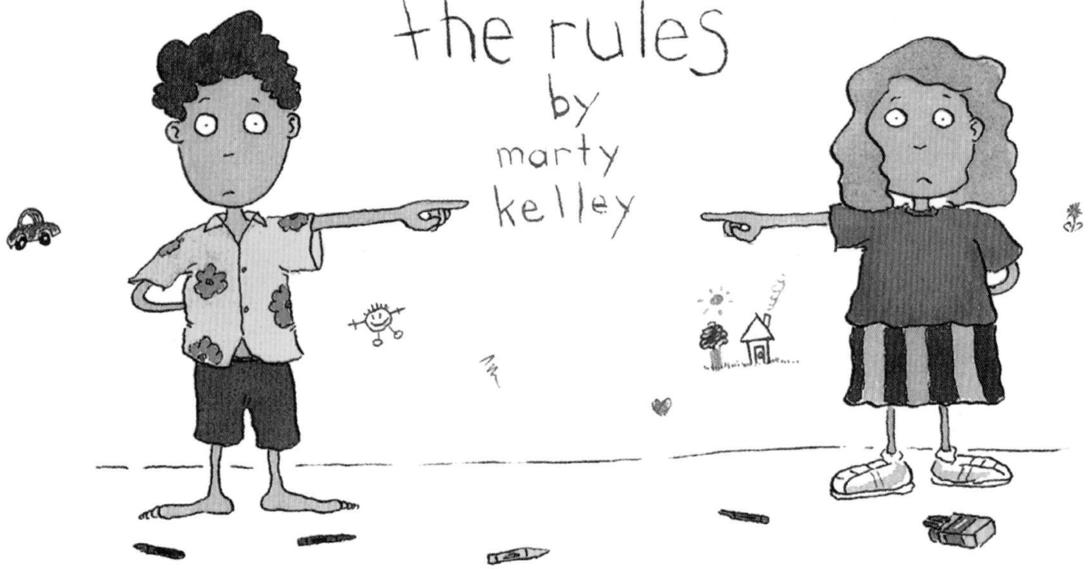

This book is for my amazing son, Alex.
I look forward to saying each of these things
to you a thousand times.

he rules
by
marty kelley

Brush your teeth.

Comb your hair.

Don't forget clean underwear.

Wipe your feet.

Don't talk back.

Don't eat dog food for a snack.

Clean your room.

Wash your hands.

Don't make guns from rubber bands.

Wipe your nose.

Don't eat dirt.

It's all fun and games 'til someone gets hurt.

Eat your peas.

Don't swear or curse.

Don't scratch, you'll only make it worse.

Chew your food.

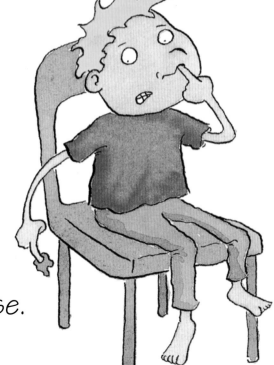

Don't pick your nose.

Don't squish mud between your toes.

Tie your shoes.

Don't be rude.

No more playing with your food.

Put that down.

Put those away.

Don't you look at me that way.

Drink your milk.

Fold your clothes.

Don't stick peanuts up your nose.

Don't make faces.

Change your shirt.

Finish your dinner before your dessert.

Sweep the floor.

Don't suck your toes.

Don't laugh 'til milk comes out your nose.

Mow the lawn.

Make your bed.

Did you hear what I just said?

Do your chores,

And when you're done,

Go outside and have some fun.